SWIM

Swim

a novel

Marianne Apostolides

BookThug | Toronto
Department of Narrative Studies No. 1

Text production made possible with the generous support of the City of Toronto through the Toronto Arts Council. Book production made possible with the generous assisstance of the Canada Council for the Arts and the Ontario Arts Council.

torontoartscouncil
An arm's length body of the City of Toronto

Canada Council Conseil des Arts
for the Arts du Canada

ONTARIO ARTS COUNCIL
CONSEIL DES ARTS DE L'ONTARIO

Laynie Browne, "Anemone," "Tongue of Woods," and "The Tower," from *The Scented Fox*. Copyright © 2007 by Laynie Browne. Reprinted with permission of Wave Books.

Lyn Hejinian, excerpts from ["It seemed that we had hardly begun and we were already there"] and ["The greatest thrill was to be the one to tell"] from *My Life*, pp. 12 and 65. Copyright © 1980, 1987 by Lyn Hejinian. Reprinted with permission of Green Integer Books, www.greeninteger.com.

Other texts excerpted: Julia Kristeva, *The Sense and Non-Sense of Revolt: The Powers and Limits of Psychoanalysis*, translated by Jeanine Herman, Columbia University Press, 2000; Julia Kristeva, *Desire in Language*, translated by Leon S. Roudiez, Columbia University Press, 1980; Jacques Lacan, *The Four Fundamental Concepts of Psychoanalysis*, translated by Jacques-Alain Miller, W.W. Norton, 1978. All attempts were made to contact the publishers for permission.

Library and Archives Canada Cataloguing in Publication

Apostolides, Marianne   Swim : a novel / Marianne Apostolides.

(Department of narrative studies ; 1) ISBN 978-1-897388-38-9

    I. Title. II. Series: Department of narrative studies ; 1
PS8601.P58S94 2009   C813'.6   C2008-907637-0
Printed in Canada

for my mother,
Frances Apostolides

Prelude

Achilles removes his shirt. Cheeks flushed, Melina avoids eye contact. She strides toward a chaise lounge tucked beside a bend in the stream; her towel slips as she steps across the plastic slats. She grasps her book. Nearby, in the shallow end of the pool, Kat's hands float down, brush against her thighs as Achilles tosses his shirt onto the lifeguard stand. Unseen, a butterfly veers past his shoulder, heading toward the waterfall. Kat hears the water's crash; she's immersed in the sound; then, just as quickly, she loses that attunement, telling herself she ought to begin. She exhales as she thinks the words, unaware that she's been holding her breath.

I should begin.

Crouched by the pool's edge, opposite Kat, Achilles scoops some water into his palm. He draws the liquid through his hair, onto his neck, which he grips, feeling the tightness. He smells the familiar scent released by this water when it meets his skin; he inhales deeper and Melina rubs her lips. She's reading a book of poetry while composing a letter to her father. She begins by describing the statue of a goddess she'd seen in the museum in Athens. She'll never commit these thoughts to written words; they will remain, perfect, only in her mind.

She misses her father.

Kat turns toward mountains that rise more severely than she'd imagined, when she'd imagined this place, which wasn't very often. Her father had rarely spoken about his childhood. In fact, he'd rarely told Kat about his past at all. They were far more likely to do things together, she realizes, now, as she adjusts her position – gathering herself in preparation. He mirrors her, she thinks; he rises then dives. He is turgid flow – away and toward – plunged in this pool where she, too – strokes – her body urged by this necessity to swim.

She swims.

Laps 1 - 13

She strokes, as taught – three strokes and a breath – and in for three and breathe on four she breathes. She strokes. She feels the liquid pass along her length – her torso, this softness, exposed to the pool's inside. She breathes, lips spread. This water, she thinks, is unusually thick – resisting her body, which swims, exerting, acting on liquid that holds her – supporting – while pulling her back. She swims – moves – and the water responds, forming reins/ cords around her chest. She didn't notice its substance/ dynamic till now – as she swims – engaging in this necessary challenge.

She contemplates the cause.

She breathes on four, lips spread – her movement through resistance – her stroke in this pool, this place where he was born. She swims through liquid, viscous, stroking toward awareness – inside this medium, unusual – she senses, now, she knows: this pool is fed by 'healing waters.'

This is the reason – this system of streams that trickle/ gush beneath the ground – inside the mountains – licking the soil's mineral core. That rock releases, dissolving its substance in water, which takes, altering internal as they – separate – slide over each other in movement and exchange. He never told her they were healing, she thinks. She read it in a book; she feels it on her skin; she sees it with eyes that are open, unstung.

She swims.

She knows, now – her knowledge given to physical/ awareness, arrived at through passage – she knows, already: she will never be healed by this immersion. Not after all she's done/ undone these last two years. She'd have to gulp the whole goddamn pool.

She swims – past him/ he whose body displaces water through force – his stroke – onto her, who swims in challenge/ engagement – he's gone.

Sorry… she murmured. She was seated, then, on the blue tile floor – that aisle in the library's depth – underground, among the stacks.

Sorry, I'm in your way…. I…

Pen on lips, legs crossed, books spread – reading some theory, expansive/ expanding – I'm in…

Barthes threw himself into interpretative writing the way others throw themselves into music, with a sense of going against the natural – against natural language, which seemed false to him or seemed to conceal the deceitful unsaid. In doing so he made (ultra- or infralinguistic) laws more fully his own, laws he considered

*indispensable to the human condition, linguistic rules conveying not
only the laws of meaning but also the body beneath meaning.*

She was conscious of herself as merging with words – made
conscious by him, whose motion drew her out.

No, it's okay, he said. I'm where I need to be...

conveying not only

...but you should be two aisles over.

She looked up, abrupt.

The assignment's due next week.

She smiled from his presumption – his assumption (already) of
the right to command | 1 |. Hello, professor, she said.

She approaches the wall – the boundary, defined – and counts,
unconscious, keeping track of her laps while recalling scenes from
elsewhere/ inside.

She recalls: he didn't reply but touched, instead, across the
spines – pausing, continuing – till he came to the book he wanted.
He slid that object from its sequence, smooth; she heard the sound
– its binding easing, opening to be read. She swims, taking air –
fast – in rhythmic breath and words: *This mirage of the body always
shimmered on the horizon of Barthes's theory, like a secret that was not apparent
but audible, signifiable...*

I'll see you in class, he said.

his voyage through the laws of language and writing. Thus to decipher

Yes, she replied – presumptuous – you will.

He paused at her voice – that sly provocation – and smiled at
her, his student – who sat on the floor, the book laid open.

She breathes on four – as taught – and in for three and up
for one – eyes open on under, she swims. She thinks: she watched
him walk between the stacks, the book in hand, a piece of paper
(white) in the pocket of his jeans. She closed her book and sat,
alone, inside that aisle – that cool blue floor – those book-walls

rising/ extending, as yet unscaled. She sensed the space around –
the dimension defined by his absence.

Absence, she considers – *ab/ esse*, 'away' plus 'to be' – to be
away – so simple, it seems, except, she questions – who is away
and from what. She swims inside that word – *absence* – the volume
originating/ erupting from that single point.

The man swims past.

He'd left the space, she thinks – that aisle where she remained,
surrounded by books – words contained/ bound – *the mirage of the
body* – he'd physically left the place they'd shared whereas he – the
other, at home, in bed – was present in body but gone – *to be/ away*
– from self. That absence had no boundary/ limit – was taken only
inside itself – protected from her physical/ touch – alterior/ other
– she who could've returned him – away – to their departure.

That night, with him — in the library, presuming – the
absence was different. 'Absence,' then, was flow/ exchange – an
effloresce – a wanting toward desire. She hadn't felt it in years, she
thinks — that lack, her needing – not since their child was born.
Until that night, she thought she'd never feel it again; in her role,
maternal, she'd almost accepted its passage |2|.

She swims, arcing toward another lap – her third – and realizes,
now, she needs a boundary – an end – a way for progression.
Without a goal – defined – she'll merely be swimming – tracing/
retracing, back and forth – remembering when she must, instead,
make a decision.

Thus to decipher

She swims through viscous – this medium, resistant – its liquid,
thick when taken on her teeth, when rubbed inside her mouth –
she swims and knows what she must do. She will swim thirty-nine
laps – one for each year of her life – and during this movement
through water, unusual, she'll arrive at her decision.

She strokes, resolved.

She breathes, uncertain.

The endpoint isn't enough. She needs a process – a way to move toward/ arrive at – take – her decision through a rational procedure. She considers, scientific: if she can specify the moment when the marriage ended – some scene (contained) – a point (defined) of 'over' – then she'll know her decision. She'll know that she'll be leaving, then, that which is already gone – leaving without severing, the attachment dead/ dried of liquid exchange. This will be her process.

She swims, searching for 'over.'

This image enables us to figure desire as a locus of junction between the field of demand, in which the syncopes of the unconscious are made present, and sexual reality. All this depends on a line that I will call the line of desire linked to demand, and by which the effects of sexuality are made present in the experience.

What is this desire?

She read, quoting to him in their aisle – that channel – the place where they'd meet (Year Two), as if by chance.

So, she said, if we take Lacan's 'Interior 8' and place it in the context of language/ literature – the narrative construction of meaning – what is this –

What, he said, do you want to know here. What's preventing your understanding. His legs were bent – arms atop knees – hands hung casually in the air, holding that pose in perfect balance.

I don't understand how… if…

You want to know what's what – define it – lock it in place: name the system, how it works, as if 'knowledge' could stabilize everything. For you, he said, knowledge means safety, stability, grasping an end – *grasping!*

He made a fist, his fingers curled, their tips in-buried, unseen.

It's not, she whispered.

You're close and it's *frustrating*, he said. I want to throttle you –
shake you into, or out of –

This image enables

Out of what...

Out of what? Out of this belief – this *insistence* – that you can
tamp things down – make things stable. There is no stable except
in movement, he said, in constant revolution in relations of desire.
There is no solid – no object or goal, an entity defined. There's
only, he said, rotation, revolution, motion.

He released his fist, as if dismissing/ disgusted.

So how, she asked, do we *create* in constant revolution?

How can we seek and feel demand/ desire – appetite's urgency,
our need for destruction – and yet, she thinks, still make a space
for nurturance | 3 |.

How can we nurture in a space of desire?

She paused.

She breathes, waiting for an answer.

She swims.

She was thinking of her daughter – aged thirteen – a child
(still), not yet able to follow her body – bleeding – into allure. How
can I... she said.

He touched her arm and opened the book. This was – then –
all the touch they'd allowed – a hand on arm in that aisle, as if by
chance.

She writes:

The desire of a subject that ties him to the signifier obtains through
this signifier an objective, extra-individual value, void-in-itself, other,
without, for all that, ceasing (as it does in science) to be the desire of
a subject. This happens only in literature. Writing is precisely this
'spontaneous motion' that changes the formulation of desire for a

signifier into objective law, since the subject of writing, specific like no other, is 'in-itself-and-for-itself,' the very place, not of division but, overcoming it, of motion.

She goes on, he said.

She does... I know.

She spoke and saw his skin – a circle – a glimpse, bound by a tear in his jeans – a hole not made in a moment/ stroke, but rather prepared over time – worn down, worn through, the white thread frayed. She looked and felt that boundary – there – the space between and urge to move – through – not cross, she thinks. It wasn't the other side she wanted. It was, instead, the slip-submission into boundary – that dimension of inside.

She swims through water – arms slicing – bubbles rising – minerals contained/ within. She feels him, now, approaching. He is a roll, a roil under her body – the water as passed from him to her in this pool, contained.

She spoke, soft – chastised – she said she didn't want to define things into stillness.

He paused.

What *do* you want, he said.

She breathes.

You, she replied, her words excessively formal: *you* know better than to ask such questions...

He bent his head in laughter: Yes... far too straight...

Non-elliptical...

What was I thinking?

She swims.

I'm thinking, she said, her laughter subsiding: I'm thinking I want that motion.

And this, she thinks, is her conclusion. She spoke those words – *I want* – and in that action/ utterance, she declared: *it's over.*

She swims, in conclusion – the marriage is over – with thirty-five laps left. Her muscles are not yet tired.

She strokes, observing her arms in exertion, propelling her forward – displacing the water – thrusting her toward the edge, its end, this place where he was born. She swims, observing – recalling through logic – that Greeks delimit this limb, through language, differently: the 'arm' extends from finger to shoulder – not separated at the wrist, thus privileging the hand, which takes/ holds – brings/ toward – touches |4|. She swims – arms arcing – feeling her body named in other ways. She senses her limb – longer, extending – and feels the water raked between fingers – that space created, the channels between – where liquid streams – rushed – because of her palm – that paddle – the pad of muscle where lines supposedly tell the future. Where once he bit, she thinks, so hungry – as if her body could nourish, constantly replenished. She watched him – eyes closed, on knees – he before her naked (upright) body: she watched him eat.

Language, he said, is logic (Year Two – Literary Theory in Contemporary Society) until it is sublime.

Sublime, she'd repeated, liking the word, its oral properties – *sublime* – though she didn't yet understand its meaning. Sublime/ subliminal/ sublimate: *limen* as threshold to 'subliminal' as under/ beneath conscious perception to 'sublimate' as transforming (directly) from solid to gaseous without becoming liquid to 'sublime' as uplifted/ unequalled.

Sublime, she'd echoed – ignorant – though now she knows.

She swims, seeing her arms as they stroke in water – their angle/ dimension – their hairs, soft, from which bubbles rise – air bound by liquid – orbs lifting toward the surface, where they will break. He's coming. She senses the change in water – the push of liquid under her torso, a displacement.

He's gone.

She swims, sublime, she knows: her hand has slipped beneath the threshold, sliding as if on language's flesh – that contoured body that offers itself to touch – to palm that slides while fingers push, not breaching the surface or slicing the boundary but causing, instead, that change of state – that under to uplift – that in-folding/ unfurling/ inversion of threshold.

She knows, she thinks: she wasn't his only student. He'd also been nourished from elsewhere/ other.

She strokes – arms extended – slapping skin on water – her sound as touch – she slaps and thinks: this isn't over. That scene in the library isn't the point, specific. She didn't embrace 'over' with her lips – not like that – not by wanting a body/ history/ man. She won't allow this conclusion, ceding control to him – that man – that power to define/ determine 'over': no. She'd turned the ground – raked the filth – before she spoke those words. Her hands had dug through wetness/ waste – that aromatic, rotting core – this body of her decision: her fingers had moved inside its cunt. She'd prepared the soil alone. She'd eaten it.

Year One – Contemporary Poetics in North America – her concession.

The choice to take this course was peculiar – illogical – especially since her writing/ thinking had always been prose. Nonetheless, she was lured by that concept – 'poetry' – drawn without understanding the source – its pull, on her – that movement/ action – her intuition (unknown) that her writing needed less/ wanted secrets. The promise that she'd find them there |5|.

'Tongue of Woods,' she began.

He'd questioned her choice, calling it unpractical.

'Tongue of Woods.'

She held the book – slim – in her hands, her body curled on the couch, her feet rubbing – together/ against, soft-stimulated, each by the other. She read:

They met upon the crimson book.

We have sung, he said, a folded hour. Impossible the way white is sand.

Color prescribes certain entrances both after, and after a reverse.

She shook her head, not comprehending: *Color prescribes...*
He sat, slumped, staring at his computer; she could see the words – their reflection, digitized – visible on the lenses of his glasses. His lips moved/ muttered; she willfully re-entered.

I must not understand you as you wish, he said, for then we would be of one body. To be of one body we could not meet.

No syllable did not seek reflection in these woods, these double companions

Until all attempts at speech resembled clouds.

Fingers entwined within what they had witnessed

Drenched was the slight lavender gray which suffuses all light, the slightly open buds of magnolia.

She broke her attention from the written/ page; she lifted her gaze to seek the words – to vision/ fantasize their meaning.
The slightly open buds, she mouthed.
Fuck! he said and slammed the screen: shut. Fuck!

She unfurled her legs – she strokes, past him – she stood and stretched her muscles. She arcs. She announced, polite, that she'd check on their daughter.

What? he snapped. Whatever – fine.

She stepped, delicate, up the stairs, one finger enfolded in the pages of the book. She didn't want to disturb him then – he, working on deadline – past – impractical promises made, spoken at the outset, his confidence swollen – tumescent – later deflating with problems not anticipated.

Her scholarships didn't pay the mortgage, he'd said, tumid.

Color prescribes certain entrances both after, and after

She walked inside their daughter's room, its light blue-dim, its curtains drawn; she looked at her girl – this child, aged twelve – in sleep.

She was curled in bed, one hand on the pillow beside her cheek; her thumb grazed her lips, plump with ease – not smiling/ speaking/ holding (withholding) – relaxed in sleep where thoughts aren't given into words. She stroked her daughter's hair that night and felt the warmth – the potent/ possible of a sleeping child.

for then we would be of one body

They'd started school the same day, she recalls – they'd sat on the streetcar side by side – both giddy – nerves bubbled into excitement. She'd auditioned – acting – for an arts-based school; her father had encouraged this challenge – hers – he aroused from his slump to give her options – expansion/ arts – a future denied to him, he said, his choices eliminated – *limen*/ threshold – banished from possibility |6|. His horizon, already, approached so close – closing around his muscle/ flesh. Horizon, she thinks, from *horos* for boundary through *horizein* to limit – a limiting circle, shackling. Horizon – hers, extending – starting school – Year One: Poetry/ concepts/ presumptive allure – her decision made, spontaneous – after – the timing right for school, she said. Now she could continue to write, bolstered by theory – progressing beyond the milky exchange of family – an exchange that was curdling then/ already, though she didn't know it at the time – that night – her fingers stroking her daughter's cheek.

She swims.

In that stroke, she thinks, she saw a change: not her daughter as an adolescent – giddy/ bubbling, going to school, breast buds forming, lines spoken as rehearsed – but rather, she thinks, her daughter as the girl she'd been – before – when she was a baby, dependence complete.

To be of one body we could not meet

An infant who understood as sensation – filling – taking stimuli into her body – sound and light as liquid/ suck. She sucked, drinking viscous, replenished by the breast – fingers floating, mesmeric in their movement through air, onto her chest, caressing – floating – her breast exposed to give the milk – her husband watching, amazed – irrelevant – regarding them with awe.

I must not understand you as you wish

She lifted her hand and stroked again – along this life, this warmth, she strokes – and in that movement/ instant, time arced forward – abrupt – and she could see her daughter as other/ another – woman: the contoured cheeks and curving lashes; the smile that spoke, aware of its speaking; the gaze and gazing. The tasting. She saw, she thinks, the woman who she – on surface – would become; the woman who – unseen/ inside – would constitute/ concentrate that which the surface must be.

Her husband swore aloud from downstairs.

She settled in the antique chair – rocking – sitting where she'd often read, aloud, to her daughter. She felt the glide beneath her weight, that familiar/ familial rhythm of slide, the lull of shush.

Shush, she'd say… Shush as she lay in her crib – crying – afraid
of sleep or, rather, afraid of entering sleep – of leaving light and
touch and mother. Shush, she'd say, then read a story – spoken,
soothing – the words not grasped as logic – discrete, defined – but
rather as sound with rounded intention – offered as maternal/
love, directly onto the body. She glided there – the girl twelve, the
Year One – and read aloud.

'The Tower'

The flower is always within the almond.

*The tower is perfectly round, of dark stone, containing only light from
a narrow window.*

The girl within dreams she is the bud, hidden by a profusion of blades.

Constantina, still enclosed, tightly folded seed. |7|

*Is the tower the seed which encloses, or is this seed the sitting room
of mind?*

She was brought to the tower unwillingly.

To follow a color not in the spectrum, a lure.

*For there to be color, she was told, while stringing a scarab onto an
amulet which she now wears about her neck, something must be
absorbed.*

One color is the absence of all others.

At that moment, all of her possible habitations vanished from sight.

One absence is the lover who displaces the spectrum.

*She feigns sleep like a curl and dreams of her past life where things
had once to be accomplished.*

And as she read, she lapped its sense – her tongue shaped
words and quenched their meaning.

The girl within dreams she is the bud

The girl within – she floated down the stairs that night: You've
got to hear –

hidden by a profusion of blades

He held one finger – up – looking at his screen until finally, she
thinks, he lifted his gaze.

What, he said: what…

She took a breath and read those lines – like almond lure in
magnolia clouds, she read.

He paused.

He squinted and asked: Am I supposed to applaud?

No – I…

Yes – you? He spoke corrosive/ acid: Yes?

I just thought…

What.

I just thought… She thinks: I just thought it was beautiful.

And this, she concludes, is the moment she seeks: not the
spoken 'I want' but the unsaid beautiful.

This is 'over.'

He's gone, beyond.

Listen, he said. In the vacuum created – that emptied space
where they could've shared 'beautiful' – he poured the sludge of his
code. His voice, she thinks, quoted letters and numbers – symbols/
punctuation – which formed the logic of 'language' online,

engineered, a 'language' with a severed tongue – not spoken but typed, not formed with cord and muscle but keystrokes/ slaps.

This code, he said, would make some simulation – he spat – of a blue ball bouncing across a website for a bank.

Listen!

His muscles were tensed on jaw and neck – bound by horizon/ eliminated options. *Listen!* He recited the symbols – the code – his face contorted in accusation, his numbness inverted to anger – vomitous – and then, she thinks, he shut (fuck) returned to numb.

She feigns sleep like a curl and dreams of her past life

The poet's words had been dispersed; her mouth was dry – the liquid in-sucked, absorbed by her body. I'm sorry, she said, lips skidding on teeth: I'm sorry – I didn't mean for this… It wasn't supposed to be…

What.

She swims, fingers wet.

I didn't mean to hurt you…

She strokes, suddenly unsure about her process – this search, scientific. She senses her uncertainty – a presence lurking – a doubt that would scatter if she looked at it, direct |8|. All she can do at this moment – this point in her progression – is note its existence and then proceed, arcing along its gravity/ pull.

I'm sorry.

Is this over.

She swims. She wants, again, the man to pass. She tries to feel his motion – their rhythm – their cycle of engagement. She calculates: their bodies traverse at different points along this pool – its length – and that, of course, makes sense: the strength of his stroke propels him through this medium/ water at such-and-thus a distance over such-and-thus a time – which (speed) can be compared to the strength of her etc. But then, she thinks, they don't just swim

as if alone; they're not isolated in this pool and, therefore, their
specific stroke – their individual – will alter the stroke of the other.
His wake, she thinks, must bounce off the side – that boundary,
hard, in set concrete – and roll back in to compound the wake that
is – always – of her on him or – she pauses in thought, this stroke
within motion. She considers: she doesn't know the physics – the
science – the laws as stated/ constructed; she knows only the laws
as enacted in the physical (body). She swims.

He's gone.

She wonders whether he noticed her – she who swims, sharing
this medium – she wonders whether he looked at her, respecting
her motion. She swims, considering: 'respect' from *specere* – to look
at – plus *re*, which means back/ again: *respect*. 'To look back at'
implies a distance – a change over time/ space – *respect* – which also
concerns appearance – *specere*, spectrum, spectre, specious – which
connotes 'seeming' and this, she thinks, is revealing. *Specere* yields
both looking and seeming – seeing and appearing – the agency
reversed, my gaze on you – your internal, given – this moment,
specific, she seeks – 'over' – specific from *specere*.

She swims in this circle, these laps, and wonders what she saw
of him, her husband, back then, at the beginning. Who was he in
her eyes, she thinks. Who was he, with his shaved head and black
goatee, wearing earrings and leather, arming himself in cultural
knowledge – high and low, distinction obscured – dazzling others
with wit and banter. She tries to recall: she remembers his hands
as he lit her cigarette that night they'd met at a party, his fingers
encrusted with paint. A canvas, he'd said: a self-portrait in grey.
He worked, he explained, with the palette knife and bare hands
– palm and fingers, the brush untouched – a technique he hadn't
planned/ anticipated – a surprise, he pronounced |9|. A gift, he
added, from whom I'm not sure…

The Muses?

Ah… the Greeks… I don't want gifts from *them*, he said and they laughed, blowing smoke, visible in its particulate grey. Her father, she thought, watching the smoke – her father would've disapproved.

'Respect,' she thinks, looking back at/ to him, from here, this distance in Greece. She swims, stroking toward another lap.

Is the tower the seed which encloses, or is this seed the sitting room of mind?

She wonders what he saw. What object/ appearance did he create of her – the woman who'd be the subject of his story – that story of him as a man – the outsider/ alone, experienced and tough in leather and piercings – a man who could attract a girl, twenty-three and tender, smart from books but innocent/ ignorant in physical experience. She didn't know, at the time, to ask who she was inside his fiction – who he was (therefore) inside her; she didn't question why he – a man, ten years her senior – would ask her to marry just four months after they'd met.

She remembers his hands – shaking – when he opened the box, presenting the ring. His fingers were clean; the lid was lined in fake white silk; she gave her assent without words.

They built, for each other, a family – a home – and they were, she thinks – happy – but never, she knows, were they violently/ joyfully ruptured into pleasure. They were always (only) agents acting on each other – subject on object then flip to top on bottom as object on subject – each riding onward, toward that climax – individual – that story/ fantasy, kept separate in their own minds.

I didn't mean…

What *do* you want.

Listen.

She strokes, in swim. She'd eat her betrayal if she could, she thinks. She'd swallow it, whole, this living being she's created. Not the lies – those verbal excuses for lateness or leaving – those tight-knit words were only lines that crossed, weaving to form a fabric, hiding the life beneath. That life, she thinks – that writhing body, reaching – wasn't the fact of sex, either: betrayal isn't copulation/ incident/ action mechanical or animal. Instead, she thinks, betrayal is fantasy – that story – the human imagination. That ability to speak one narrative while living another.

She swims.

Shush.

She strokes and kicks – and in for three and breathe on four – she breathes, lips spread. Her mouth – *no syllable did not seek* – is voracious, widening like a snake but – no – that's the wrong image, she thinks. That image comes from words/ lines crossed: snake. She focuses, now, on the physical/ foundation of the metaphor.

She breathes.

The feeling has a rim like lips – their supple edge – but the motion isn't a jaw. The mouth, instead, is sliding, stretching – the lens of a camera – dilation, expanding – but not a camera's mechanical progression. The motion, she thinks, is like birth: her mouth |10|.

You'd better go without me, he said.

It was Year Two – one year ago – fourteen years after they'd met, the portrait (grey) hanging on the wall. I've got to finish this job.

You're not going to come? She crossed her arms, her chest expanding beneath the fabric – the air in-taken, engaged in this challenge. We're supposed to go together… You've never met my colleagues, my professors…

He leaned on the table – arms spread, shoulders hunched, cornering his laptop. You seem to do fine without me, he said. He stared at his screen, reading the code as written.

all of her possible habituations vanished

You realize, she said, this is my graduation. My Master's celebration… You realize –

I realize, he said, what this is.

She slammed the door: shut.

Fuck.

One absence is the lover who displaces the spectrum

She was waiting that night at the transit stop when she saw the woman across the street, standing in the window of her second-hand shop, arranging some clothes on a mannequin. There, in the window, dressed in casual – faded jeans and leather belt, a tight/ cropped shirt – that woman embodied female ease, the sensual contained – separate/ secret – not needing to be displayed. The woman, then, reached to adjust the mannequin's clothes; as she did, she recalls, her T-shirt lifted, exposing the curve of her body, that softness near the belt.

The streetcar was coming.

She let it go.

She swims through water – her aisle/ channel – she strokes, in memory. The man is past.

Try this on, the owner said, peeling a dress from its hanger. This would look really good on you…

She took the dress – smiling, grateful – and lay her purse on the change-room chair. She stripped the outfit off her body, aware of her nakedness – bare except for her panties (silk) and high-heeled shoes that opened her pelvis – tentatively – back. She stood in awareness, unseen, and draped the new dress on – streaming – falling toward the ground like water off an edge. She felt her form.

She slipped around the change room's curtain, walking toward the full-length mirror – watching herself walk toward (herself), that dress in linger-step to slide. She didn't notice the cut or colour; she saw, instead, the spray of fabric – the froth around her ankles and up – the single slash, parting/ closing along her thigh – her hips firm-bound, carving a space through air – dip on side through centre and over – dipping/ carving to centre/ point – a figure eight lain/ eased to horizontal. She saw, in that mirror, her body/ self not as subject or object but rather, she thinks, as motion.

She swims.

You *must* buy this dress, the store's owner said. Her hands came to rest atop her ribs, her fingers on the fabric |11|. A professional touch: the touch of a woman who deals in garments – in bodies clothed. She touched, assessed – stepped back to see; she nodded once, arms crossed beneath her breasts.

Is it okay? she asked. She posed like a girl – like her daughter, she thinks. Like her own child, playing a role – pretending with costume and script – filling her body with need/ emotion whose consequences remain, only, on stage.

Am I… Is it okay? she repeated.

The woman put her hand on her hip, bare above the belt. They looked at each other – seeing – safe in their casual game. They paused, in breath – she breathes – then overflowed in giggle-laugh, a sparkling in their female pleasure: this draping playful/ truthful deception.

And this, perhaps, is the moment she seeks – this sensual without sexual, this erotic that's given as gathered, fulfilled in itself. Perhaps this was 'over.'

She swims, uncertain.

The tower is perfectly round, of dark stone containing only light from a narrow window

She strokes, in viscous water – mineral/ thick.

She was brought to the tower unwillingly

He's gone.

She wishes she could tell him, she thinks. She wants to speak/ confess – lay herself bare before him – he who was harness/ grip on reins, who drove her, hard.

her past life where things had once to be accomplished

He who – in that same motion – gave her the possibility of release.

She swims.

She wonders if he would've chastised her.

She strokes through air – her arm/ hand, fingers/ palm – and locks into language, conscious hold: 'chastise' and 'chastity' come from same root – that same radical – *castus*, the word for pure. From 'chastity' as purity – comes – 'to chastise' as punish (especially by beating) – comes – 'to chasten' as refine/ purify – and this, she thinks, is absurd, as if it – that punishment/ beating – could purify/ cleanse, excoriate want – the filth that's in her mouth and through her sex.

The desire of a subject that ties him to the signifier obtains through this signifier an objective, extra-individual value, void-in-itself, other, without, for all that, ceasing

She wants his chastisement, she thinks; she wants someone – other – to have the power to forgive.

She kicks and strokes, she breathes – voracious – she sucks in air, she needs to stop. She'll take a break, she decides, at lap thirteen |12| – one-third, exactly proportional – a short break to disengage and build her strength, to interrupt this circular motion. She swims, resolved, and sees the man approach – his chest, defined, the muscle in exertion/ against. She looks at him again – a young man from/ of this place, these healing waters. She swims past, re-entering 'respect.'

She realizes now – in this movement toward pause – that she'd fantasized him – her professor – envisioning 'him' as an object of knowledge – an other/ man constituted by learning/ ideas – a man who'd fill her through logic/ words. She saw herself as seen by him – his student, wanting – she who strove for him/ he who would, in turn, drink her excess – drowning, open-mouthed – his body submerged in her need to please/ achieve – a need that spilled from her, giving him pure. She'd allowed that dynamic, she thinks. She didn't want him as subject – he – individual, possessing a story/ history, drive/ desire. She wanted – in truth – her teacher as a means for her release.

How can I…

You're close and it's *frustrating.*

She swims in water – here – and considers 'over.' This word possesses various meanings, depending on its function. As adverb, 'over' means completely through, from beginning to end though it – 'over' – also means as preposition or adjective, always with a sense of exceeding/ traversing/ permeating – 'over' – describes direction/ constitution/ relation – 'over' – is lain across the surface, spread through till excess – 'over' – onto the other side.

Is this over?

Shush.

The mass of doubt is now dispersed: her process was flawed, the question ill-defined. She won't locate that moment, specific, since 'over' doesn't exist as an object, unchanging. These moments she's recalled – these scenes, interactions – they signify differently, depending on her perspective – this vantage/ point that is her body/ being, which isn't solid or stable but changes through time, propelled by the self's undeniable rhythm.

There is no stable except –

These laws indisputable to the human condition

And yet, she thinks, she seeks finality/ totality – the seduction of meaning – *over*. She seeks and eschews, rebels when she approaches. This she knows from him – her father – he who believed he held meaning in his body, so strong and trim; he who refused fate – a man who ran, carving a path from history – here – believing he could start again/ over – beginning as if his past didn't surge in his muscles/ core. She swims in this pool, this place where streams once coursed in his mouth as the water he drank and the food he ate – the succulence of fruits, the bitterness of leaves he gathered during war; these pools and falls where he once splashed, learning his body through action/ motion. This is where he was boy, then, and now he's gone.

She swims, in pool, in Greece, alone. She strokes. She swims from core – from place that is beneath/ below/ adjacent to that spot, that 'non' that always eludes because, she thinks, it's a hole – a lapse – a force of driving start. Of there – for him – she swims.

He's gone.

She strokes once more, seeking the edge |13|.

First Interlude

Kat's body comes to rest immediately. Her legs float down, scraping against the unlined wall. The sting is gentle; it's a kiss almost, a man's unshaven face. A reminder of the world out there, outside this pool.

Kat will pause only for a moment. She wants to catch her breath, that's all.

Achilles continues to swim.

Kat turns, extending her arms on the pool's ledge. The stone marks a warm line across the top of her back; her legs sway effortlessly, dangling in the pool's depth. She closes her eyes. The sun meets her face directly now; orange spreads across her vision, constantly morphing into various shapes. Occasionally she senses a coolness in this colour; the cause, unknown to Kat, is a butterfly that passes overhead, casting a shadow.

We see only the leaves and branches of the trees close in around the house. Those submissive games were sensual. I was no more than three or four years old, but when crossed I would hold my breath, not from rage but from stubbornness, until I lost consciousness. The shadows one day deeper. Every family has its own collection of stories, but not every family has someone to tell them.

Melina is utterly lost. She'd never admit that to her mother, especially not with this book that she'd found two weeks ago, on the eve of their trip to Greece. The collection, *My Life* by Lyn Hejinian, had been placed on her mother's bedside table, atop a book for her dissertation and beneath her latest journal.

Melina continues to read.

Without what can a person function as the sea functions without me.

The water rises on Kat's chest, lapping against her skin. She opens her eyes as Achilles turns a somersault, pushing hard against the wall. His body surges forward, into his next lap. Kat observes the easy strength, his muscles eager and untested. Achilles' is a youthful beauty.

Kat looks away; the light is too harsh in its reflection off the water.

Through the windows of Chartres, with no view, the light transmits color as a scene. What then is a window. Between plow and prow. A pause, a rose, something on paper, of true organic spirals we have no lack. In the morning it is mauve, close to puce. The symbolism of the rose depends on its purity of color.

Melina rubs her lower lip, her finger sliding back and forth. The movement is unconscious.

The red rose in its redness leaks no yellow. In other words, it develops the argument.

Melina's finger stops. She contemplates the phrase.

Kat is gazing at the mountainside. The landscape, when viewed from below, is a canvas of browns, muted and various. From her position in the pool, Kat can't detect the caves or streams that flow toward the waterfalls; she can't see the wildflowers, either, with their spray of colour. These mountains seem inert, though she knows this is untrue, if only because of a story her father told her once, years ago.

The symbolism of the rose depends on its thorns.

This village is called Loutra or 'Baths,' an appropriate name, given its most distinctive characteristic: the pools of water that gather beneath six small waterfalls whose progression forms the perimeter of the village. At the outskirts of Loutra, the mountain's underground waters breach the rock's surface; these disparate streams rapidly merge, tumbling together in the first fall. As that water pounds into the rock bed, it forms a natural pool whose boundaries can't contain the liquid, which ceaselessly overflows, spilling into the next stream that runs toward the next fall, where it tumbles, and so on. The large, man-made pool is filled with water siphoned from these streams. The water is said to be healing, due to its specific, naturally occurring combination of minerals.

"The symbolism of the rose," Melina whispers. She feels herself speak the words: her lips spread on 'S' then press in a line of 'M' to split on 'B'; her tongue touches her teeth on 'L' for one quick tap then pulls back, shy, to sound her breath on her vibrating cords at the end. Her directors have often remarked on her ability to articulate words clearly, with precise diction and emotion. Her mother has noted this too, though Melina becomes angrily embarrassed when Kat makes that kind of comment, even if they are in private.

"The symbolism of the rose," she repeats, but now it's just a mouth and teeth. She shakes her hair over her face.

Achilles strokes faster now; the water is more furious around him. Kat senses the change. Her muscles become alert, her body preparing, filling with tension. In one smooth sequence, Achilles plunges out of the pool – the water cascading off his body, splattering onto the ground – and Kat pushes off the edge. As she enters her first stroke, she sees a stunning figure lying on the chaise lounge – her body long and lithe – her hair curtaining her face, revealing her lips, which she rubs – slow – soft on the membrane.

Kat swims.

Laps 14-26

She feels the stroke on her skin – the sweat washed off, in-mixed with this medium, the water of this pool. She swims toward fourteen, that hard-edged boundary, then back toward more, that oval motion (laps) elliptical/ slit. Fourteen, she considers, feeling the image spread through her muscle: her daughter's body – elongated/ supple, readied for touch – awaiting that impress/ impression that must come from other: force. Fourteen.

She anticipates the damage.

She swims.

She was fourteen when it began, she thinks, if 'it' is disorder/ behaviour itself. If, though, 'it' is luscious terror – the 'I' alone, standing, feeling that awful draw toward sex-hunger-speak – that desire toward loss that pools/ fills: if 'it' is that dynamic, then 'begin' was always. Is never.

She swims: begin.

She recalls that moment, specific, when damage/ touch offered awareness – that moment when memory could create itself in words. She knows because she spoke it to him, who asked, the night it began.

What's your first memory, he said. He nuzzled her hair and took her scent – polluted – into him.

They lay in bed, on humid sheets, their limbs and histories intertwined – tangled in confusion. Her head was resting on his chest; her finger traced a line across his torso, sensing the irregular smoothness of a scar.

I was in the bath, she said, and my mother was washing my hair.

She put a towel on my face, intending to keep the soap from my eyes, then she dumped the pitcher, full, on top. But the towel got wet; it covered my mouth and I couldn't breathe. The pitcher, she told him – her finger on scar on side over hip – the pitcher was plastic.

I remember the smell of the plastic.

She remembers, now, the sense of smother – the fabric sopped, sealing her mouth – a gag that pulled tighter the harder she sucked – she breathes – stifled by the towel, held by her mother. Who was, she thought (then) – as she spoke in his bed – attempting to keep the soap from her eyes. Who was, she knows (now) – as she strokes in this pool – enacting a ritual of them, together – singular – them in that moist room. The tile was green.

I remember…

His arm was snaked around her back; it pulsed atop her muscle – a twitch to prompt/ encourage, she thought at the time – to ease her forward, signalling that he remained beside, following her memory. She continued.

My mother leaned over the tub, she said, trying to grab my arms – my wrist – but I flailed, slid, frothing the water… She couldn't keep hold so she screamed instead – *stop* – as if the sound could control.

She paused, her legs constricting around his limbs |14|.

She sucked in breath and screamed again – repeated/ incanted the word – *stop* – that hit the tiles and bounced back in, toward her, to fill the room – that moist container – with palpable sounds, those intersecting, not-quite lingual, fully articulated shrieks.

Stop!

Her mother's nightgown was splattered with water. It stuck to her skin – belly and breasts – rippled, she said and he didn't respond; it rippled as she breathed, chest heaving in anger at me – at us, she corrected – at what we were to each other. *With* each other, she thinks.

In each other.

She swims.

So that's my memory, she said, my first; that was the night it began.

His clock was glaring on the bedside table; its time was neon – numbers red – dots flashing their seconds, insistent, that mocking beat of digital duration.

I must go home, she said and dragged her nail atop his scar.

Yes, he responded. He kissed her mouth. Yes, you should go…

Home.

She swims.

She's strayed too far, she thinks. She needs to re-engage with her decision – the question – this freedom has led her nowhere. How, she thinks, can I ever return.

A metaphor, she resolves: if she can find the metaphor for their marriage – the likeness that shapes a visible image – conjuring a picture, depicting complexity otherwise gnarled in useless words – if, then: she will know what to do. Her decision will be obvious – observable – revealed by the simple figure of speech.

She swims, seeking a metaphor in this land of myth and symbols – signs and bodies – stories lacking linear progression, webbed across gods and mortals, nymphs (nubile) aged fourteen.

Her arms arc through water – healing – fed by streams on this border, mountainous, between Bulgaria and Greece. The Balkans, she thinks, breathing out – breath through lips in water and up – to air – *the Balkans*. She hears her breath pass through her lips – a burble: the Balkans – they've taken their name from Vulcan, she thinks, the 'B' in Greek that sounds like 'V,' from Vulcan (Balkan) – Vulcan, the Roman god and also the Greek: Hephaestus, he was originally/ in his origin, here.

She swims, recalling her studies – Year Two: Classical Mythology in Modernist Writing – Hephaestus/ Vulcan, the first-born son of Zeus and his wife, the legitimate heir. A god often mocked though never maligned – a boy who limped, ill-formed at birth; a son who loved his mother lamely, lacking eros – wedded, ironically, to 'Love' (Aphrodite), that sea-foam goddess who rippled as want. Balkan/ Vulcan/ Hephaestus: the Olympian son, the husband to Love, the god of metal: he, Hephaestus, worked in a forge, shaping objects/ tools through fire, stoked and coaxed to rising – mastered – flame controlled, allowing the start of civilization/ culture. 'Hephaestus,' she repeats |15|: 'Hephaestus' from 'Vulcan' from 'Balkan' from lips and he, she thinks, would've loved her deduction – that lingual logic-sculpt she couldn't make till now, in swim. She needed to travel here, to Greece – this physical/ place – in order to know.

She swims, in Greece, where he was born. She needs, she thinks, a metaphor.

She breathes.

Maybe the marriage is an object, forged – an alloy of merged components, shaped – a homogenous molten pour whose properties are solid/ stable: strength and bind – plasticity, play – contour and angle, lustre and sheen: all that's allowable in this – the figure – is contained within its alloyed properties, forged at its founding – historical – that moment of begin.

She swims, stroking toward the hope that she's found her decision: her marriage as an object/ tool, forged as he – lame Hephaestus – had done and now she's (already) deflated.

This will not work.

This metaphor is flawed.

A marriage as an object would be an idol: a false god to whom they'd pray – a material/ mystical figure they'd created at their moment of coming/ together – their origin – but this, she thinks, allows no room for change/ motion. This figure allows only for different forms of worship.

She swims, harder, within frustration. She wants to be over; she needs to make a decision. She swims with arms and legs but mostly with gut – with muscle, gripped, which doesn't move yet propels. She knows, from him – from how he moved but also, she thinks, from explicit instruction: once.

Strengthen your core, he said. He stood at the pool's edge – she inside – on his rare day off. He would, today, teach her how to swim.

What? she asked, confused. She didn't expect him there, near her, gazing down: commanding.

Strengthen your core, her father repeated.

He held a glass, the liquid crawling up the walls, around the chunks of ice.

Okay, she said. The chlorine, she remembers, stung her eyes, the tender tissue – pink, exposed – around the rim. Okay.

She heard a splash of laughter – loud – from the others who frolicked, distant, in the pool's shallow end. They were guests at the party – a 'Pool Party' at the home of another Greek, an entrepreneur who'd made his fortune off tampons (slim) and nipples for the bottles of babies. His wife – his third – wore strappy shoes on her well-groomed feet; her white shorts cut one line, straight, at the level of her pubis; her halter top was red.

Her mother was home with a headache, she thinks – with the word, at least. I've got a headache, she'd said that morning, after breakfast, reading a book by Updike or Cheever. Her father sighed – the sound as evidence, aural, of plans ripping – a rift sundering his hopes for the day. She offered, then, to take her mother's place |16|; she was, she remembers, eagerly accepted.

We won't stay long, her father had said on the car ride over.

Whatever you want, she'd replied. She sat up front, her bathing suit tight beneath her dress. Usually, she thinks, that spot – that seat – was reserved for her mother. Whatever, she repeated, and shifted her weight.

She swims – she swam – away from the others. She'd needed some goal – an object/ objective – and so she swam.

She'd found her father at the edge of the pool, unexpected.

Okay.

The core will girdle you, he said, keep you straight, keep you going. Let's go let's go – let's see you swim.

She swam/ performed – she girdled her gut – she stroked for her father.

She reached the end – the shallow – where the others played. He was, already, there.

So here's what you're gonna do, he said.

She clutched the edge, her shoulders hunched – legs in-slipped between her torso and the wall – her knees to nipples, pelvis (tucked), curving the base of the spine. She shivered there, her body unprotected by layers of fat. Even then she was skinny – abstaining – denying though denial lacked harsh implications till later – fourteen – when she started to want with tissue that bled.

First, he said, you breathe on four – not two – on four: it's faster, he said, if you swim like that. He abandoned his glass on the lawn that seemed to tangle in vine up the outside, concealing.

So, he said. You breathe on four.

He bent at the waist, stroking through air; he looked aside and opened his mouth, his lips out-splayed, emphasizing the suck. Then he turned his head – down – into the space that was, supposedly, water.

In for three and breathe on four, he said, he breathed – lips splayed, muscles taut – body in simulated swim, resisting the fantasized water.

In for three and breathe on four.

Okay?

She watched him from her huddle in water.

Behind were the guests, cavorting; in front was the carcass of a lamb, roasting and spun, steady, by a boyish man with a thin moustache.

You breathe on four –

She watched her father stroking, sincere, talking/ teaching – unaware of others around – of men with golden chests and silver hair; of women whose bikini tops winked to cover their breasts. She watched and saw, beyond, the wife who sipped her drink and peeled a layer of meat off the flank; she bit and smiled at the man – her laughter made flesh for him, his boyish – those red halter breasts, that body that moved: steady.

She splayed her toes along the wall, the smallest outstretched – further, reaching – until she sensed her tissue (thin), that web that dipped between the digits |17|. She watched – she smiled – she pushed her pelvis onto her heels, a smooth long pressure/ impression – until the skin threatened to tear.

She liked that threat, she thinks as she swims; its danger was familiar from earlier.

We won't stay long, he'd said.

She swims.

Do you see? he repeated. You breathe on four – eliminate the excess – any extra motion will cause delay, slow you down. Do you see?

I see.

Let's try again.

She swims in the pool – in streamlined (fast), in strength from her core – which as he taught she took (extreme) in please/ in pleasure for him, her father, who stroked —instructed/ modelled/ moulded the flesh of satisfaction – challenge/ achieve – engage beyond the threatened tear.

Let's go! She heard him shout when she tilted her head – the breath on four – she heard his encouragement/ criticism – clear: Let's go!

Faster.

She swims.

Now, he said, as she reached the edge – he'd jogged along, to the other side – okay.

Was it better, she asked. Did I do –

Your breath is right but your core is weak.

My core…

It's weak.

He removed his shirt, impassioned – lost – taken inside this sacred act of teaching. Your core is here. He slapped his torso, beneath the pit of umbilical sever: your core is here.

She saw the hard pelvis – bone – the muscle-draw toward triangle's tip and then, above, the symmetry – compartments – under his skin, the centre/ divider drawn, thick, by solid muscle. Your core – here – this is your force. He spoke. She watched. You swim from here.

She nodded her head.

You don't understand, he said. He swiped his shirt off the deck.

I do! she protested. 'You swim from your core' – that's what you said!

Right, he said. And what does that mean?

I don't…

You don't… no.

She swims, feeling her failure – his deep disappointment – she lay inside that spill. I'm sorry…

Her father laughed gently. There's no need to be sorry…. He crouched down low, down (close) to her. I'll teach you, okay? I'll teach you tonight – I'll show you how to build the muscle – properly, he said.

Okay – tonight. She shivered in the pool.

'Cause sit-ups are hard, if you do them right.

I'll do them right.

You'll do them wrong. He stood and slapped his gut again: flat. But, he added, I'll teach you how to do them right.

Okay, she said. You'll teach me: tonight.

And what, he challenged, will sit-ups achieve?

They'll strengthen my core; they'll give me force |18|.

And what, he asked, will you do with that force?

I'll swim from there.

Good girl, he said.

She smiled.

Good girl… Now let me see you swim.

She swims.

She breathes on four – three strokes and a breath – and in for three and up for one and three plus one makes four, makes pace, makes rhythm of her swim, which she learned, from her father, who revealed – when he taught – what was already there.

Here.

Let's go!

She considers the guilt she's carried – hidden – this acceptance that she's to blame – alone – for their situation, the necessity of her decision. Her father, she recalls, was the only person who'd questioned their engagement – the marriage, so soon after they'd met. He, more than any/ other, knew she craved revolt and release, constraint and achievement of loss.

Are you sure this is what you want?

I want that motion.

She swims, asking herself who was to blame. Did he efface her first, erasing her from his illumination; did he ask her to act, luring her toward other through his absence. Or, she thinks, did she entrap him – shackled, bound by obligation – and then escape those strictures/ commitments. Who was written out of whose story; who was the author of this narrative – their tale, complete, with wedding and cake, the child well-loved, a home and health – normalcy, stability – entry into the grand narrative, safe in that house.

And this, perhaps, is the metaphor she seeks: the marriage as a house, a home they'd built. This structure – home – is container and volume – boundary and (therefore) space. She swims, elaborating the metaphor; she strokes through its logic. Their marriage/ home: they'd determined the placement for windows/ light, the secret corners, the doors (internal) that led from room to room; they'd established the sightlines – obscured or extended – created the angles for vision/ perception, the possibilities allowed or denied. Here, she thought, she could be independent – working/ writing – yet breathing his scent and sighs, the creaks as he moved; here she could take him – individual – into her. They built this home, she thinks, lacking knowledge/ intention, unskilled in erecting such a complex design, they – unwitting – left negative spaces – vacuous channels – through which the air could flow: air and therefore scent and sound. The air/ exchange travelled in paths unpredicted: columns – vertical/ horizontal – bends and leaps, traversing gaps: her room might be in private correspondence with another – remote – at the back of the house, allowing each other to sense their sighs as if they were close – as if they could know the cause of those sounds.

I know what this is.

Stop.

She swims, considering that other home – her first – the green tile and porcelain tub, the dining-room table where they – together – enacted their ritual, the bathtub long outgrown. Age fourteen she was when it began – this ritual expression of primary relation – her engorged connection with her mother |19|, a relation she tried to starve. Each night, she thinks, she placed food in her mouth and chewed without taking – not swallowing – not letting it into her throat – that passage to the body, its blood.

She swims, she breathes, she blows the air in water.

Her tongue was then the reverse of suckle. It undulated, strong, her nourishment – out – and into the napkin she'd brought to her mouth. Her mother would watch.

Why are you wiping your mouth? she'd ask each night, those words turgid with all unstated. Why – her father would protest: There's no problem! he'd say/ implore. He'd speak from fatigue, the weariness of this inevitable – this pattern he didn't construct as ritual/ significance but only as action/ words taken direct – true and denoted and, therefore, denied.

Without the ritual, this scene must've been merely/ terribly bizarre.

Why…

She brought that bundle of food, uneaten, onto her lap – that threshold, wet, where words were entered – wanted – waiting, she was, with swollen lips to hear.

What have you done.

She strokes with arms – those arms that once were bird-winged bone and tendon, stretched – unseemly in their awful lack of muscle/ fat. A girl she was – eighty pounds at age sixteen, this body (the same) that swims.

Eighty pounds, she thinks: stop.

She sat across from her mother, facing the kitchen, where the garbage rotted beneath the sink.

Funny, her mother would say, she thinks. That word would be an opulant pearl, formed from the pressure in her throat and up – regurgitated – given, then, into her mouth and dropped, gorgeous, off her lips. Funny, she'd repeat: the dog was sniffing through the garbage last night, as if it were filled with food.

Funny, she'd echo, her eyes on her mother in an unctuous gaze that said: Say it.

Say what I have done.

She'd sit in her chair each night, she thinks, her jaw tight with hunger for food – her lips soft in excited fear that she would say – it – the all of 'it,' that couldn't be contained in logic. Say it with your body's mouth, she thought/ she wanted.

Strange, she'd add, she thinks.

Strange and then she'd tilt her pelvis (open) onto the seat of the chair; she'd feel that touch – full – her tissue pressed to the wood: Say it – strange – I wonder why.

She strokes, enraged.

If she could open her mouth and paddle the water into her face she would, she thinks. She wants to do that: she wants to turn her rage into a scream – inverted – a scream as suck of water – in – but still a scream, she thinks |20|. Still a rupture from her chest and through her throat – a scream as a motion of non-cohesion – the self becoming plosive mass, projected through her mouth and throat, its chunks and grain in-floating and felt but not cohering into sense. She'd scream and take this water into her body to fuel her rage and rein it, too: to shut it tight – her scream as rage as suck – to make it come to rest inside her core.

Disgusting, her mother said as she rummaged through the garbage each night: disgusting.

She swims.

She thinks: those nights she'd lay in bed, alone, and count the objects – calories, eaten – food as numbers and rule of logic. Her hand would rub her body – her belly – her only flesh that lacked a ridge of bone; she'd rub in circles near that threshold – coarse – that kinked hair her fingers broached, on occasion. She'd lay in dark those years, anorexic. The other, now, would lick her, full. It would come at night and tongue her body – too exhausted/ thin to resist – it – the hunger that came like a mouth on her sex except it ate inside of her: a mouth *inside* that bit, engorging, every night while she lay in bed, her head extended back – body arched – waiting for that opening.

She swims.

This was her history – her story, entwined – she never persisted in asking for his. She should've known, she thinks. She should've intuited him – his desire – his need to succumb to struggle, internal, without other/ exchange. She couldn't compete with his depression – that seduction – the motion on his own sex – bestial – his body's desire led into its own tongue – teeth clamped – bloodied on language's muscle. She couldn't lure him from this sadistic lover who knew when to coddle and when to mock, speaking sweetness as the ropes rubbed his skin, tying him down – his failure at art, his shortfalls at work, his wife whose sex wasn't fulfilled/ fulfilling – a lover who whipped him, penetrating his numb.

She could've responded differently. She could've made a different decision.

I'm where I need to be.

She must return, she thinks, to the question she's posed: what is the metaphor for their marriage. She's conjured metaphors for other dynamics but none, she thinks, that have led her toward her decision, necessary: what is the metaphor.

It was a surprise – a gift.

She strokes in this water – this viscous liquid – Balkans/ Vulcan/ Hephaestus – and he, she thinks, was also betrayed. He, Hephaestus, had heard from Hermes, that fleet-footed male, the messenger god who brought him news: Aphrodite and Ares – his wife and brother, Olympian gods of Love and War – of pleasure and aggression – were fucking in the marital bed.

This she recalls from Year Two – Modernist Writing – her

mouth expanding.

He made a net inside his forge |21| – a net of chains so fine they couldn't be seen, there, strung across the bedposts – poised above, preparing to ensnare those bodies, unclothed. In lame stillness, Hephaestus hid and watched the bed – his wife and brother – bodies, moving – a coupling that gave birth to Eros. He hid and watched the net come down.

She wonders, then, if that might be the metaphor for the marriage: a net strung between two poles – people, separate – who change, grow, experience over time, alone but connected by threads, strong and fine, with space for light and breath. A net that transfers the pull between – desire or need – or catches a body in fear or failure; a net whose tension translates emotion into force, physical, from one to the other, but also has substance – touch/ materiality that can hold or be held.

Yes: the net is the metaphor.

And if the net is the metaphor – the relationship they've made – then she must determine its strength, dimension, the size of its gaps, the slack between. And if she can identify those properties – the ones that they, together, had forged – their net/ relationship/ metaphor – then she will know.

She asks herself, then: what did they forge.

She recalls those days when they linked their hands, rubbing her belly, its curving softness where their child grew, her limbs moving within; she recalls, too, the gaps in their stories/ histories – the information not said at first and then (in time) hidden/ held from the other.

Respect/ *specere*/ to look at again: let's go.

She swims, in Greece, in Balkans/ Vulcan/ Hephaestus, she strokes.

He slept in that bed, she thinks – those sheets – and knew

she'd been there with others. He slept and imagined that net –
forged – pressed against his muscle, which grew harder with this
image – this thought of her with him, in bed, unclothed, their
rhythms: betrayed. He felt those chains bind him lush, lashing:
that net he'd made, alone.

The gods laughed, mirthful.

She imagines, now, her own arms arcing through ensnarement –
a fine-wrought net fallen around her body, which moves; an
object/ figure – foreign – yet formed by her own mouth: this net
of words.

I want – sublime.

This figure enables

Her muscles are turgid with this progression.

She won't pursue this course anymore. She swims, recalling
the theorists' logic: the metaphor is a figure from a different era –
bloated with meaning – an era of truth and transcendence, of one
secure story, told with authority: stable. She will not conceive of a
metaphor. She needs, instead, a different plan; she needs to make
a decision.

I need to make a decision.

She's said those words for months, she thinks. She doesn't even
know what they mean anymore |22|.

She swims.

I guess you leave tomorrow, he said as he sat, surfing the net.

Well – yes, tomorrow…

And after?

And after… she said. After: I don't know.

He nodded. You realize I resent this.

What, she said. Say it…

The fact that you're taking her away from me.

She swims, now, deconstructing her response – her careful

creation of reasons/ excuses to visit his homeland, so needed after his death, she said: before her dissertation, during her birthday – the timing just right for her and her daughter who will, she said, become too old, too adult, to want to travel on a trip, together, this journey with her, to their homeland. I've wanted to take this trip for years, she added.

He nodded. Yes, he said. You take your trip – you seem to be taking a lot these days.

And what do you mean, she said, by that.

To which he replied: I have work to do.

Her indifference, then, was swept away – the sheets pulled off, exposing her anger, her energy toward. She wanted, she thinks. She wanted – like the goring of her cunt by his cock – she wanted some confrontation: some grapple within the covered known. She wanted to shout the problem – her betrayal, his depression, her hatred of this, her loss (complete) of belief and trust and faith in him/ her/ them – and love and honour and family/ vows. Her loss of self as she'd defined: a woman/ mother/ wife, not tainted by the lingering smell of want.

She swims.

I need to pick up a few things, she said. At the school.

The school, he said. I see.

You do – I know.

She went to his apartment, her blood prepared by him – her husband – he held her down, his hands as cuffs locked hard on her wrists. He pinned her arms on the pillow; she responded as struggle – her muscles sculpted through exertion/ engagement, her honest attempt to force herself free. With his weight astride her hips, his palm on her wrists, he bent to take the tissue that once gave nourish. First he licked and then he teased and rolled it, dense, between his teeth. She stopped her flailing, fearful, knowing –

anticipating – the pain. He held her body in gazed command, his mouth on her breast; he held and must've felt her breath – her breathing – in the wave of her panic. He paused |23|. He smiled, she thinks, his lips widening around his teeth; he smiled before he clamped his jaw and bit.

She swims.

She strokes, her muscles now moving as biceps and traps and pecs near her breasts, all moving in one true motion, which is her body as she swims, in this pool, in Greece.

She strokes.

She screamed, she thinks, in rupture and rage; she screamed as he drank her loss.

I need to make some decisions, she said once she'd washed off his scent. He was lying in bed, his legs thick trunks; he didn't respond.

I think he knows, she continued and – quick — he became electric/ alacrity; propped on his elbows – eyes on her – he spoke his instinct, his question: the first.

Does he know who? he asked.

Does he know – ?

Does he know it's me?

I need to make some decisions.

She swims.

She strokes in water – the Balkans/ Vulcan/ Hephaestus – here, the place of his birth and also, she thinks, the birthplace of her – Woman – Pandora, the first. She was formed by Hephaestus, shaped in deception – in and from and for deceit – since she was the figure, curved, of punishment. She, Woman, was made by the god for the fact that he – Prometheus – stole fire, a flame that was less an object/ substance – a thing, taken – than a means for transformation. The ability, she thinks, to master force, making

culture and progress – art and history – civilization, controlled by
skill.

She swims. She considers. She's lured by the promise of this
myth – the truth it might reveal if engaged by her mind. She
continues.

Good girl.

Prometheus, she thinks, wasn't punished by a woman but
by, instead, a beast of prey. He, that male, was tied to a boulder,
shackled tight at ankles and wrists, his body bare so every night the
creature – eagle – could come to land – its talons scraping against
the rock and he, the male – the one who stole – would lift his head
in agony – knowing – and watch that magnificence dip its mouth,
ripping his flesh and drawing the sinew, out. In pain he'd scream
and then – succumb – he'd lower his head, submitting to this – the
act of being taken.

For him, she thinks, this was punishment; for mankind, however,
the punishment was Woman/ Pandora as shaped by Hephaestus,
as ordered by father. He, Hephaestus, the husband to Aphrodite/
Love – he knew the form: that curved shoulder and sinuous band
of muscled (back) to centre (cunt), the under of into and up toward
her rounded belly beside her pelvis/ bone, the patient weight of
her breasts, her nipples with their dense sensation, and onto her
neck with pulse and quicken and mouth: he knew.

Lame Hephaestus took this knowledge and made.

She swims.

And once he'd coaxed this woman from clay and water – here –
he gave her, naked, to female gods who clothed her in deceit:
jewels and gown and honeyed scent; voice and gaze and painted
lips – allure – they blessed her with this: woman.

She swims inside this liquid progression – Pandora-betrayal,
fire-Love, Hephaestus-theft, desire-War, Eros-beast – she swims

and needs to make a decision |24|. She, woman – who walked in linger-step to slide, who moved as punishment/ chastisement – she plagued him, urging Man to abandon his need for culture/ laws – arts/ implements – meaning: controlled. She, Pandora, possessed a secret. This secret couldn't form as words; it was, instead, held by lips – her moist edge/ rim that dipped inside, into the body/ possibility of desire.

She swims.

She needs, she thinks, to twist herself into alignment – the comfort of numbers – aged sixteen and eighty pounds.

Aged sixteen and eighty pounds.

Aged sixteen and there she is, safe in the cling of numbers/ calculation, their hard precision/ solid unambiguous. Aged sixteen and eighty pounds she was, she strokes, toward lap – toward number/ goal – thirty-nine/ eighty pounds – as if 'eighty' could signify her belly's shape, skin plunging off sternum, sticking to her spine's ridge, her ribs winged out in frightened scatter – or – her blood meek, insipid, lacking mineral to hold its thick, its smearing – or – her hunger not as muscular need but rather as panic, frenzied along her nerves as now as – *now!* – as shrieked from central/ primitive knowledge that her organs are dying. As if 'eighty' could convey.

She swims.

At age fourteen – the age of her long-limbed daughter, lounging poolside, reading in the shade of a tree – at age fourteen 'it' (disorder) began; at age sixteen 'it' (action) inverted – a fist and finger were stuck inside, ripping the disorder up her throat – through her mouth – scalding the sensitive tissue of her speech as she was emptied. They were/ she was (she thinks) so different on the surface – these motions – as if it – the surface – were the core of truth.

She swims toward end.

She's tired, now, remembering that moment – then – its specific exhaustion – that seep-fatigue, the blood-tired titrated by premonition/ pre-thought of change, impending. She felt it that day, the begin. She was aged sixteen and eighty pounds when she ascended the stairs – two at a time, as her father had taught – and stepped into the hall.

Her sight was clear only at the centre – a dot that extended, deep, surrounded by the play of light – of pinks and greens in dazzling blocks, strobing, forming the walls of a funnel, its surface refulgent in neon non-friction. This vertiginous suck was familiar: every time she stood or moved, she felt this sordid illusion – the challenge to remain upright and moving.

Disgusting.

She couldn't compute what she saw – there – in that tunnel at the top of the stairs: a dress swaying/ gliding through air, high off the ground |25|.

She paused, she breathed, she waited for that sickly strobe to clarify/ cohere – to let her see the truth of this odd vision. She breathed and touched the wall; she balanced and Oh! she said – actually – oh! She remembers that: the word said, stated to herself, alone. She spoke her comprehension. The dress, she saw, was hung on a hanger whose hook was placed on the edge of the door. The door, she thinks, had eased – open – unable to seal in its frame from that obstruction – the hanger whose arms gave the dress its illusion of shape.

Am I…?

Her shoulder pressed on the hallway's wall; her chin dug – hard – on her collarbone's stick. She stood, crumpled within deprivation – her lack of food and blood, her fear of corruption – of heeding her appetites' swells. She stood and watched that dress glide, long, through the air.

Can you get me the towel? her mother said. Her voice was rounded, edged with moisture. She lay inside that room – beyond the door – taking a bath in the porcelain tub, preparing for the party that night.

I forgot a towel… Can you bring me one? She moved in the bath; the water dripped against itself, its droplets lapped by the pool, contained.

She listened to the echoed distortion of water.

She was dying.

Her muscles were eaten by her own body, her jaw internal.

Aged sixteen and eighty pounds.

She got a towel from the closet.

Thank you, her mother sighed. Her breath was a moan – the sound of pleasure, oral – such lushness in the looseness of her cords.

Thank you…

She paused beside her mother's dress. She looked at the form in water, reposed; she saw the contours – the body rising, soft, over that threshold of liquid, moving as she breathed – the weighted sway within the slow unstill of water. She watched her mother and slipped her fingers inside the dress.

Her hand was wicked by the fabric – up/ taken – she watched her mother – the silk of the dress like liquid pouring over her palm – she reached and watched – and higher, her arm inside, drowned by the lining, her mouth wet – she saw her mother's hair, dense in its thicket – that darkness teasing – concealing.

Thank you, she murmured.

She strokes, arms arcing, hair slick from the speed. This pool is warm on her body, the rim of her lips – this breath is round from her mouth: a murmur.

She swims.

It began in the house that night, alone. It lasted eight years, she thinks – that binge and purge, that gorged release – that 'it' lasted eight years. Eight, exact, till her daughter was born in her body – her cells in-sewn, their food shared directly by blood – its pulse – their mouths pristine and pure.

She strokes one last time then opens her eyes and lips, her hand gripping the pool's edge |26|.

Second Interlude

"Excuse me."

"Me?"

Achilles laughs. "You," he says. "I'm wondering what you are reading. It looks very interesting."

"It is! It's a book of poetry. *My Life* – I mean," she quickly adds, "it's not my life. It's a book of *poetry* called *My Life*, by this woman – " Melina trips over the words. She turns aside, locking her gaze on a butterfly that circles furiously in the turbulence above a waterfall.

"I understand," Achilles says.

Melina smiles, turning back, thankful.

Kat watches her daughter flirt. Her heart is contracting with tremendous force, having swum twenty-six laps, half of them in constant interchange with the young man. She looks at his torso, recalling the statues in the National Archaeological Museum in Athens. He could've been a model for those sculptures, excepting the shape of his nipples that point down, like teardrops. The ancients would've considered this a flaw.

"Are you liking it?" Achilles asks. "This book?"

"Yes! I mean... it's very sophisticated."

"Sophisticated, I see... And Loutra? Are you liking this? It is not so sophisticated, I think. But very beautiful."

The water has evaporated off Achilles' skin, leaving a mineral taste. He'd discovered that phenomenon as a boy, when he'd swiped his forearm across his lips, wiping away the juice of an apricot. That mineral taste, mixed with the fruit's warm sweetness, felt somewhat sinister. On occasion, after, he would suck on his forearm at night.

"Are you also a poet?"

"No, I'm an actress." Melina is surprised by her assertion. It's true that she acts – she'd played the lead in *Antigone* that spring, winning the part over older girls at her arts-based high school. That decision caused quite the controversy among her classmates, and more than a little difficulty for Melina. "Yeah," she repeats. "I'm an actor."

Achilles nods. He puts his hand on the edge of the chaise lounge, beside Melina's thigh. He assumes she's seventeen years old. Sixteen or seventeen, her body firmly curved at her cheeks and breasts but stretched long everywhere else. He guesses, correctly, that she's a virgin. The thought passes quickly, brushed aside. Achilles wipes his lips, removing his hand from the chair. He is nineteen years old, home for the summer, filled with the expectations of his parents. He still hasn't told his father he's decided to major in the Classics, with a focus on classical political thought. His father wants him to be a banker.

"You certainly have the beauty to be an actor," he says.

Melina's breath rushes forward, leaving a painful hollow in her belly. "I'm still in school – I mean, I'm not a professional or anything…"

"But you will be," Achilles declares.

"I what – I will…? I…"

Achilles laughs sympathetically.

"What!"

"Nothing, it's just…"

"What…" Melina shuts her eyes.

"I'm sorry," Achilles says, lowering his body to peer in her face. "I think I forgot to introduce myself. My name is Achilles." He extends his hand.

From her position in the pool, Kat sees that first moment of contact – the offered smile – receptive. She watches, now, the reverberations ripple from her body – the waves spreading, expanding from her, who moves, diving toward her next lap.

Laps 27 - End

She swims, arms arcing – three strokes and a breath, she breathes – mouth open on inspiration/ air – and in for three, through water, resistant – and now she knows: she can't stop this progression. Her decision is inevitable; she fears only its arrival.

She swims.

This is beautiful, she said. They stood before the ancient goddess – an idea/ force contained in form – this artist's attempt to create sensation, communicate sense. The museum was crowded.

Who is it? her daughter asked, caressing her arm with her palm, unconscious. Who's it supposed to be? She tried to find the placard, but the Greeks were sloppy with signs/ words that explained, concrete.

The goddess, Aphrodite…

Her daughter shifted closer. It makes you want to touch it, she whispered.

What…

They paused, together: still.

What makes you want to touch. What do you see.

Her daughter's head tilted, left; she composed her body in contemplation.

There's no right response. I'm just wondering what you see – what you perceive – when you look.

She looked, again – respect/ *specere* – it's the clothes, she said.

Her dress was diaphanous – rippling over breast and belly – hugging her thighs to dip in the space between. The figure amazed her – delicate though shaped from solid.

Explain, she commanded – teaching as she'd been taught.

It's the way the clothes cover the body – but don't… not really….

Would it be different, she said, if the goddess were nude?

Her daughter's lips pressed in a smile – hers, alone – the pleasure internal at this, her discovery. I wouldn't want to touch it, she said. Her body eased as she spoke – her muscles softening, curving away from rational/ thought.

I wouldn't feel that (secret) compulsion.

Good girl.

It's beautiful, she said.

She swims.

She's beautiful.

Swinging her sundress, she drifted away, walking amidst the crowd that gazed on torsos and limbs, the fabric diaphanous – deception/ allure – these female figures shaped to punish – chastise – taking into awful purity.

Sorry, she said, and giggled as she bumped into a man.

No worries, he replied, his accent roughly London. I was just looking…

The crowd in-filled the space between; she couldn't see her daughter or apprehend her words, specific; she could only hear the laughter – that clarity – rising above the din of voices.

I'm where I need to be.

Is it okay?

She wandered through the gallery – alone – drawn to the frieze of a lion attacking a deer. Its jaw was locked around its back – claws digging lines in skin, gripping, muscle bulging – a hungering master devouring its prey whose lips were open. She gazed at the deer – its neck no longer tensed in struggle, its eyes widened without seeing. She sighed, then, and heard the moan – the sound that breathed its knowledge, come – the knowledge that it was being taken.

Thank you…

When they left the museum that day, she thinks, they passed a row of lilacs, blooming |27|. Their fragrance, unctuous, coated her mouth as she breathed.

I really liked that, Mom, she said and skipped – just once – a girl, bleeding, aged fourteen. She twirled in her dress – the fabric, thin, rippling as she stretched her arms – reaching as if to take her mother's hand.

She must've sensed, she thinks – 'sense' from *sentire*, to feel, from *sensus*, the faculty of perceiving. 'Sense,' she considers – stroking through water, its thickness on skin – is the boundary/ touch between self and world – the means to absorb the outside in – sensation – and organize it into knowledge – sensible.

She must've sensed, she thinks, the change in the home – their house – that net of words – *I know what this is* – language overheard or seen, scrawled, in that privacy beneath the book of poetry.

I'm sorry.

The girl within dreams she is the bud, hidden by a profusion of blades

She's young, arriving on the cusp – bleeding/ wounded by that movement – her motion along the boundary/ rim – *sublime,* she said – the secret that she would soon inherit.

Stop!

On four, she breathes; on one, she notes a pattern/ rhythm: her eyes are open for three – while under the water – but closed above.

She breathes, on four – eyes shut in air, then – open – for three on under, she swims, aware.

She sees the water cut by light – refracted by the prism – the substance itself – which peaks with her – her stroke – her motion in this, the viscous unusual. She swims. She decides, now, to try a change: she'll keep her eyes open on air and closed in water – and open on four and closed for three, she takes this decision, discrete/ defined.

Listen.

The bubbles rumble out her mouth – for three – and then she breathes – a breath – her in, her eyes are open. She sees, now, the sideways mountains. Their trees are horizontal – growing toward horizon – reaching for the column of sky. She swims and in and wants (again) the breath of up – the stroke sideways – her interest scientific. She didn't expect this shift – this world as tilted from altering her eyes – her plane of perception – her body in liquid/ swim not upright/ upstanding as was, she thinks, the norm.

We won't stay long.

She swims, she strokes, she opens on up and sees on – breath – then closes for three and thinks in dim, in dark, in blue: the planes

of axis intersect – the lines of sight and solid objects interact in
their play of perception – her lips, his clock, the title (horizontal)
on the vertical spine, the face inclined to read.

I'll teach you, tonight.

She sees the mountains and from this perception – strange – she
senses the mountains different/ unusual. These godly structures –
the Balkans/ Vulcan/ Hephaestus – aren't solid/ concrete but are,
instead, alive with motion – eaten as eating – consuming without
depletion – their waste grotesque in its sweetness, taken. These
mountains, she thinks, are writhing with streams and roots –
growing/ effluent – predators/ prey jawing in nourishment –
joyful/ moist – the jaws and fingers wet.

She breathes on four – on up she sees – the mountains' caves –
that blackness/ negation – the all-absorptive colour of loss where
surface is scraped, becoming interior/ entered – that place, she
thinks, of mouth.

There's no problem!

He told her, once, about this place |28|. Just once, a story. A
scene of him, here, in Greece – this village, these mountains – this
water where she now swims. They were together in the kitchen –
he and she and her daughter, newborn, just two days old. She was
screaming – her baby – her mouth a cone, that hollowed space,
amplifying the voice, desperate. It surrounded her body, she thinks;
that voice merged her inside to out.

The sound never changes, he said and smiled in sympathy.

Oh god, she moaned, don't say that – please…

Her father, she thinks, was fixing the door to the porch out
back. His tools were strewn on the kitchen counter – screws and
drivers, pliers, mallets, all with their function/ purpose defined,
deeper to him than to her, who didn't know the tasks and tools
– the ways in which they fit. She saw him take an awl in hand;

he positioned it, precise, in the frame. With a rhythmic pause, he tapped until the wood curled, assuming the shape of a wave before its crash. When the coil was complete, he scooped his finger in the gully that remained, allowing the latch to properly fit.

She opened her mouth, her lips wide-spread.

Her husband, she recalls, had promised to fix the latch 'soon'; she was, when he spoke, merely five months pregnant.

He swiped his finger.

Oh, *she'll* change, he said. She'll change so fast you won't know where it went.

He blew in the hole, scattering the sanded wood. But the sound, he continued: the sound of newborns – *that* doesn't change. That sound is the same with all of them, he said. He stood – upright/ straight – and gazed at her – his daughter/ mother – the one who knew (intimate) without explicit. She doesn't make her own sound yet, he said, soft.

She screamed.

Her mind, she thinks, clicked on that scream: she was seized – crazed – a tensed cord flicked. She grabbed her daughter's skull, her fingers spread; she tightened her grip on that softness, there, beneath the ears/ beside the bone. In snap/ release, she shoved the mouth onto her breast and pressed – in – holding. Her daughter bucked. She struggled with her tiny body; she didn't care. She held that skull and plugged that voice like a fist in the mouth. The sound was swallowed.

She panted; she breathes.

Let me take her, her father said and washed his hands in the kitchen sink.

She heard the liquid, dripping.

Thank you…

It never changes, he said and swayed. His cheek nuzzled her

scalp; he breathed her in – touched her supple.

I remember this sound, he said, from years ago. From Greece, he continued, when I was a boy |29|.

She tasted the dust – that sanded wood, warm as if alive on her lips. She pressed those lips together – inside – against her tongue.

I remember… it's clear. The sound is clear, but it was so long ago…

He told her, then, about the caves – here – those caves she spied as she breathed on four – eyes open to see.

We hid in the caves, he said – all during the war… the wars, he corrected – we'd flee from the village and hide in the caves. It was, he said, she thinks, protection.

He swayed, rhythmic.

We hid from the Nazis at first. Then others… the rebels, the Greeks, the government, guerrillas… I didn't know who but men… always men… who came and so we left our homes and hid in those caves. He paused. In Greece. You should see them someday, he said, he swayed, eyes closed. You will: you'll see them someday, when you're ready…

She breathes.

But there was a baby… an infant who wouldn't stop crying. He shushed her now and swayed and shushed – his legs wide, eyes closed – his lips were dusted with maple. She watched him sway into story.

It was that first time, he said. The Nazis were coming… that's all we knew. And so we left… we fled for the caves… an entire village climbing a mountain… climbing and hiding in a goddamn cave.

It was cold, he said. More than dark… that's what I remember…

The cold, she thinks.

He paused. He kissed the silence – her calm – his voice through chest, a vibration to her – this child, now/ still, listening to the story, soothed by its telling.

Shush.

She wouldn't stop crying, he said. We heard them shouting… coming up the mountain…. There'd been a raid, I guess, he said. Some soldiers were killed… some Germans by Greeks… and she wouldn't stop crying. This kid… this one kid… this baby, so loud…

And then…?

And then there was just the sound of water… one drop at a time… falling from the ceiling of the cave. It was relentless, he said, his arms enclosed on the body of a baby. It was… he paused… I would've screamed too, he said; I would've screamed if I hadn't started counting those drops – one drop at a time – thousands I counted… Thousands, for hours or days – who knows how long – I just kept counting.

I was afraid to let myself stop, he said.

She breathes, on four, she breathed: she swims.

He's gone, she thinks. He's gone in stroke, his vessel – burst – to flood the brain with blood. He loved her, she thinks: her to him in him as her she swims – he's gone – he loved her as her own subject/ self. She swims in this pooling rupture of him – his rhythm – she swims, within.

It'll go so fast, he said, he swayed. He kissed her supple |30|.

She swims – now – eyes open on up. She kicks and strokes – she slaps the water with arms and ankles – with limbs, she slaps – she feels that rigid command: the need to touch him again, now gone.

They lay in bed that night, she thinks – the day her father had told his story – they lay in bed, all three.

Their daughter, she thinks, was crying – again/ still – she didn't know what to do. She looked at her baby, this alien/ other, this child – her – birthed just days before, this infant, her mouth, the sound – needing/ invoking – and she trying (failing) to respond.

What do I do, she said, aloud... What am I supposed to do...

Her husband stirred. Can I help? he said, half-asleep. Do you need...?

No, baby, she said. It's okay... you sleep...

She touched him then – his shoulder and back – reaching across the gulf where their child lay. You sleep... She drew her finger across his skin – gentle, she thinks – they were gentle with each other then. They were hopeful – held by history, cyclical – mother/ father/ child they were – roles, identified – 'mother,' 'father' – she made them so – she, whom they'd made, this child – 'family' they were, from her.

I should go home.

He loved her – exclusively, exquisitely – he loved her.

He always gave his laughter/ engagement – his knowledge and open – to her, their daughter. There was, between them, the truthful exchange of excitement. She saw without resentment, she thinks: even as he disappeared from her, she saw/ respected – them together, giving/ exchanging – presence.

Is it okay...?

It's beautiful.

You sleep, she repeated. You sleep, my sweet.

She soothed him then – caressed his skin – though she was bruised from the labour/ birthing – the fluid pooling, swelling her form in odd asymmetry. Her cunt was oozing with clotted blood, the hair tangled and sticky; her breasts were hot with angry engorgement, the milk compacted in nodes that bulged beneath the skin; her nipples were parched, dotted with blisters, red and refulgent, filled by blood, raised by the power of her daughter's suck.

She was wailing – hungry – smelling the food/ her – not yet released.

You sleep, she said.

She lifted her daughter off the bed. She needed water, she recalls. It was, she thinks, a driving need – this need for water, a goal so simple – this need that brought her down the stairs, clutching the baby, frightened she'd fall – that echoing wail – the mouth-cave opening, tongue quivering – the sound in darkness – but she was moving.

She was moving, she thinks.

I need a drink, she thought, as if the water could heal.

She drank, in gulps – the water dribbling out her mouth, dripping on her baby's scalp. She squirmed and screamed, her mouth a hole – no teeth – just tongue and funnel.

That sound never changes.

There are snakes in my body, she thought |31|. She looked at her breasts – terrible – filled with ducts like snakes who'd swallowed prey – whole – swallowed and vengeful they were, in her, her hard breasts, those snakes engorged.

My god... she seethed.

She screamed, in hunger; he'd counted the drops; her daughter was placed on the breast.

My god...

It came without arriving.

She was – now – liquid.

I need to make a decision.

She shuts her eyes in the pool of water. She feels the panic – disorientation – location removed, the guidelines gone – seeing nothing but black, swarming. She swims in this pool – this mineral/ origin – swimming despite her panic – this inability to measure her progress – logical/ rational – a decision, undeniable. She keeps her eyes closed. She breathes through panic, reined; she strokes, in darkness.

Good girl.

She relapsed, she thinks, following his death: she returned to binge-and-purge – revolt/ release with food (alone) – not offering/ receiving the challenge with others – with language/ words or bodies/ muscle or history/ stories that pushed and shaped, asking of her, commanding a response/ exchange.

He's gone, she thinks.

He's gone... he's gone... Those words were repeated – incanted – he's gone... Her mother told her over the phone, the phrase like a bubble, popping off her lips: he's gone. She didn't name the subject – speak the predicate – she uttered, instead, her wet lament – her meaning direct/ immediately conveyed. Without words, she thinks, she understood: she felt it, heavy, the steady press – that realization – he's gone.

The relapse lasted eight weeks – eight, exact – beginning on the night of his funeral – ending the day of her invocation.

Mommy... she heard her daughter cry, curled on the couch with her mother, a widow, lost in confusion – the rules ripped apart, their story shredded.

Mommy... she cried.

She paused and panted on the bathroom floor, her incoherence splattered on cheeks and chest, her neck and lips.

Mommy...

I'm here, baby, she said. I'm here.

She swims.

They cried on the couch that day, all three. They were held

inside this huddled body, sharing their grief – this truth – their tears and limbs, slick, liquid smeared in hugs and moans – from me to her, our liquid need to fall within – tasting and sucking this blood – direct – our voices spoken as knowledge, non-verbal.

She breathes on four.

She decided, that night, to return to school – a decision not made from logic/ will – from rational thought – but rather revealed through her body's arc – an awareness lifted toward gliding arrival, propelled by her rhythm: allowed.

She swims, she strokes, she breathes on four. She's now aware of the change: she'd altered her pattern, flipped to norm – eyes open on under and closed on up – and open on down and closed in air. And open.

Your core is here.

She slaps the water.

I need to state my decision.

She hasn't reached her goal, she knows – that number, defined – but the goal no longer has meaning. She's already done the work, she thinks. There's nothing more to do but open into its pleasure |32|.

Postlude

"Give it a name," Achilles says. He holds a butterfly in his palm; its wings are still wet, preventing it from taking flight.

"A name?"

"*Tó ónoma.*"

"*Tónoma?*"

"No," he laughs.

She laughs. Her shoulders lift as she giggles. They are painted with a brushing of freckles. "*Tó ónoma,*" she voices.

"Beautiful. You speak beautifully. *Oreaía.* You must be a beautiful actor."

"*Tó ónoma.*" She repeats, perfectly.

"Beautiful – *oreaía.*"

"*Oreaía.*"

"Yes."

The butterfly's wings are starting to pulse, drying in the sun. Their colour is delicate, washed almost clear. Melina wouldn't have noticed its subtle beauty if the creature hadn't been held in this man's hand.

"You must be quick," Achilles says. "It's going to fly soon. And if you don't name it before it leaves, it doesn't really exist."

Melina takes her task seriously. "I don't know what to name it," she says. She watches the wings pulse.

"Close your eyes. Close your eyes and give it a name."

Melina clamps her eyes tight. "Okay... but... what's it called in Greek?" Her eyelids flutter with the effort to stay shut. "In English it's called *butterfly*."

"Butterfly – yes," Achilles says. "In Greek: *petaloútha*."

"*Petaloútha.*"

"This means petals in flight."

"*Petaloútha*," she says. "Petals in flight."

"Keep your eyes closed." He touches her eyelids with the tip of his finger. She doesn't giggle.

Kat looks at the expanse of the pool, which she has traversed thirty-two times. She lowers her body and opens her mouth; the water flows inside.

"Give it a name."

Kat holds the liquid beneath her tongue, tasting the minerals. She tries to loosen her throat but her muscles resist.

"You must be quick!"

"But I don't..."

"Quickly!"

"Oh!"

Kat hears a gasp of delight and turns to see: Melina is seated beside the man, their shoulders touching. Together, they are watching a butterfly's wavering flight. Kat perceives Melina's purity of wonder – her joy at sensing the unnamed possible. She watches her daughter and feels the opening – her muscle relaxing, allowing. She takes the water through her throat. She lifts her arms to swim.

Notes

The book Kat reads during her visit to the library in Laps 1-13 is:
Julia Kristeva, *The Sense and Non-Sense of Revolt: The Powers and Limits of Psychoanalysis*, translated by Jeanine Herman, Columbia University Press, 2000.

The book Kat quotes to her professor in Laps 1-13 is:
Jacques Lacan, *The Four Fundamental Concepts of Psychoanalysis*, translated by Jacques-Alain Miller, W.W. Norton, 1978.

The book the professor quotes to Kat in Laps 1-13 is:
Julia Kristeva, *Desire in Language*, translated by Leon S. Roudiez, Columbia University Press, 1980.

The collection of poetry Kat reads in Laps 1-13 is:
Laynie Browne, *The Scented Fox*, Wave Books, 2007.

The collection of poetry Melina reads during the interludes is:
Lyn Hejinian, *My Life*, Green Integer, 2002.

Acknowledgements

These words are too slight to carry the fullness of my gratitude toward my family: Fran and Jim Apostolides; Athanasia and Romeo Walters; George Apostolides and Colleen Roney; Lucy Grigoriadis, Sophia Grigoriadis, and John White. You are my stability, solace, and joy.

I'd like to thank the owners, staff, and fellow patrons of Alternative Grounds café in Toronto, where creativity flows amidst the chaos. Thanks, also, to the Toronto Arts Council, whose financial support helped put food on the table while I concentrated on this work.

A great heartfelt-cheer is sent to the BookThug Nation – readers, writers, and editors alike. You are why this is. A few people need to be named specifically: Martha Baillie and Mark Truscott, whose early feedback and ongoing encouragement were (and are) essential; Stuart Ross, whose generosity is matched by his skill; Jenny Sampirisi, an editor who gave this book her intellect and understanding, and with whom I feel privileged to have worked; and Jay MillAr, who allows risk to happen. Finally, thanks to Keva, who reminded me.

Colophon

Manufactured in an edition of 500 copies in January 2009 by
BookThug. Distributed in Canada by the Literary Press Group:
www.lpg.ca. Distributed in the U.S. by Small Press Distribution:
www.spdbooks.org. Shop online at www.bookthug.ca.

BOOK
PRODUCTION
WAR ECONOMY
STANDARD

Cover images by Melanie Gordon: www.melaniegordon.com
Book + Cover Design by Jay MillAr